Printed in the USA

A Midsummer Night's Dream

By William Shakespeare

Contents

Persons Represented

THESEUS, Duke of Athens

EGEUS, Father to Hermia

LYSANDER, in love with Hermia

EMETRIUS, in love with Hermia

PHILOSTRATE, Master of the Revels to Theseus

QUINCE, the Carpenter

SNUG, the Joiner

BOTTOM, the Weaver

FLUTE, the Bellows-mender

SNOUT, the Tinker

STARVELING, the Tailor

HIPPOLYTA, Queen of the Amazons, bethrothed to Theseus

HERMIA, daughter to Egeus, in love with Lysander

HELENA, in love with Demetrius

OBERON, King of the Fairies

TITANIA, Queen of the Fairies

PUCK, or **ROBIN GOODFELLOW**, a Fairy

PEASBLOSSOM, Fairy

COBWEB, Fairy

MOTH, Fairy

MUSTARDSEED, Fairy

PYRAMUS, THISBE, WALL, MOONSHINE, LION; Characters in the Interlude performed by the Clowns

Other Fairies attending their King and Queen
Attendants on Theseus and Hippolyta

A MIDSUMMER NIGHT'S DREAM

ACT I

SCENE I.   Athens.   A room in the Palace of THESEUS

[Enter THESEUS, HIPPOLYTA, PHILOSTRATE, and Attendants.]

THESEUS

Now, fair Hippolyta, our nuptial hour

   Draws on apace; four happy days bring in

Another moon; but, oh, methinks, how slow

This old moon wanes! She lingers my desires,

Like to a step-dame or a dowager,

Long withering out a young man's revenue.

HIPPOLYTA

Four days will quickly steep themselves in nights;

Four nights will quickly dream away the time;

And then the moon, like to a silver bow

New bent in heaven, shall behold the night

Of our solemnities.

THESEUS

        Go, Philostrate,

Stir up the Athenian youth to merriments;

Awake the pert and nimble spirit of mirth;

Turn melancholy forth to funerals—

The pale companion is not for our pomp.—

[Exit PHILOSTRATE.]

Hippolyta, I woo'd thee with my sword,

And won thy love doing thee injuries;

But I will wed thee in another key,

With pomp, with triumph, and with revelling.

[Enter EGEUS, HERMIA, LYSANDER, and DEMETRIUS.]

EGEUS

Happy be Theseus, our renownèd duke!

THESEUS

Thanks, good Egeus: what's the news with thee?

EGEUS

Full of vexation come I, with complaint

Against my child, my daughter Hermia.—

Stand forth, Demetrius.—My noble lord,

This man hath my consent to marry her:—

Stand forth, Lysander;—and, my gracious duke,

This man hath bewitch'd the bosom of my child.

Thou, thou, Lysander, thou hast given her rhymes,

And interchang'd love-tokens with my child:

Thou hast by moonlight at her window sung,

With feigning voice, verses of feigning love;

And stol'n the impression of her fantasy

With bracelets of thy hair, rings, gawds, conceits,

Knacks, trifles, nosegays, sweetmeats,—messengers

Of strong prevailment in unharden'd youth;—

With cunning hast thou filch'd my daughter's heart;

Turned her obedience, which is due to me,

To stubborn harshness.—And, my gracious duke,

Be it so she will not here before your grace

Consent to marry with Demetrius,

I beg the ancient privilege of Athens,—

As she is mine I may dispose of her:

Which shall be either to this gentleman

Or to her death; according to our law

Immediately provided in that case.

THESEUS

What say you, Hermia? be advis'd, fair maid:

To you your father should be as a god;

One that compos'd your beauties: yea, and one

To whom you are but as a form in wax,

By him imprinted, and within his power

To leave the figure, or disfigure it.

Demetrius is a worthy gentleman.

HERMIA

So is Lysander.

THESEUS

          In himself he is:

But, in this kind, wanting your father's voice,

The other must be held the worthier.

HERMIA

I would my father look'd but with my eyes.

THESEUS

Rather your eyes must with his judgment look.

HERMIA

I do entreat your grace to pardon me.

I know not by what power I am made bold,

Nor how it may concern my modesty

In such a presence here to plead my thoughts:

But I beseech your grace that I may know

The worst that may befall me in this case

If I refuse to wed Demetrius.

THESEUS

Either to die the death, or to abjure

For ever the society of men.

Therefore, fair Hermia, question your desires,

Know of your youth, examine well your blood,

Whether, if you yield not to your father's choice,

You can endure the livery of a nun;

For aye to be shady cloister mew'd,

To live a barren sister all your life,

Chanting faint hymns to the cold, fruitless moon.

Thrice-blessèd they that master so their blood

To undergo such maiden pilgrimage:

But earthlier happy is the rose distill'd

Than that which, withering on the virgin thorn,

Grows, lives, and dies, in single blessedness.

HERMIA

So will I grow, so live, so die, my lord,

Ere I will yield my virgin patent up

Unto his lordship, whose unwishèd yoke

My soul consents not to give sovereignty.

THESEUS

Take time to pause; and by the next new moon,—

The sealing-day betwixt my love and me

For everlasting bond of fellowship,—

Upon that day either prepare to die

For disobedience to your father's will;

Or else to wed Demetrius, as he would;

Or on Diana's altar to protest

For aye austerity and single life.

DEMETRIUS

Relent, sweet Hermia;—and, Lysander, yield

Thy crazèd title to my certain right.

LYSANDER

You have her father's love, Demetrius;

Let me have Hermia's: do you marry him.

EGEUS

Scornful Lysander! true, he hath my love;

And what is mine my love shall render him;

And she is mine; and all my right of her

I do estate unto Demetrius.

LYSANDER

I am, my lord, as well deriv'd as he,

As well possess'd; my love is more than his;

My fortunes every way as fairly rank'd,

If not with vantage, as Demetrius's;

And, which is more than all these boasts can be,

I am belov'd of beauteous Hermia:

Why should not I then prosecute my right?

Demetrius, I'll avouch it to his head,

Made love to Nedar's daughter, Helena,

And won her soul; and she, sweet lady, dotes,

Devoutly dotes, dotes in idolatry,

Upon this spotted and inconstant man.

THESEUS

I must confess that I have heard so much,

And with Demetrius thought to have spoke thereof;

But, being over-full of self-affairs,

My mind did lose it.—But, Demetrius, come;

And come, Egeus; you shall go with me;

I have some private schooling for you both.—

For you, fair Hermia, look you arm yourself

To fit your fancies to your father's will,

Or else the law of Athens yields you up,—

Which by no means we may extenuate,—

To death, or to a vow of single life.—

Come, my Hippolyta: what cheer, my love?

Demetrius, and Egeus, go along;

I must employ you in some business

Against our nuptial, and confer with you

Of something nearly that concerns yourselves.

EGEUS

With duty and desire we follow you.

[Exeunt THESEUS, HIPPOLYTA, EGEUS, DEMETRIUS, and Train.]

LYSANDER

How now, my love! why is your cheek so pale?

How chance the roses there do fade so fast?

HERMIA

Belike for want of rain, which I could well

Beteem them from the tempest of my eyes.

LYSANDER

Ah me! for aught that I could ever read,

Could ever hear by tale or history,

The course of true love never did run smooth:

But either it was different in blood,—

HERMIA

O cross! Too high to be enthrall'd to low!

LYSANDER

Or else misgraffèd in respect of years;—

HERMIA

O spite! Too old to be engag'd to young!

LYSANDER

Or else it stood upon the choice of friends:

HERMIA

O hell! to choose love by another's eye!

LYSANDER

Or, if there were a sympathy in choice,

War, death, or sickness, did lay siege to it,

Making it momentary as a sound,

Swift as a shadow, short as any dream;

Brief as the lightning in the collied night

That, in a spleen, unfolds both heaven and earth,

And ere a man hath power to say, Behold!

The jaws of darkness do devour it up:

So quick bright things come to confusion.

HERMIA

If then true lovers have ever cross'd,

It stands as an edict in destiny:

Then let us teach our trial patience,

Because it is a customary cross;

As due to love as thoughts, and dreams, and sighs,

Wishes and tears, poor fancy's followers.

LYSANDER

A good persuasion; therefore, hear me, Hermia.

I have a widow aunt, a dowager

Of great revenue, and she hath no child:

From Athens is her house remote seven leagues;

And she respects me as her only son.

There, gentle Hermia, may I marry thee;

And to that place the sharp Athenian law

Cannot pursue us. If thou lovest me then,

Steal forth thy father's house tomorrow night;

And in the wood, a league without the town,

Where I did meet thee once with Helena,

To do observance to a morn of May,

There will I stay for thee.

HERMIA

         My good Lysander!

I swear to thee by Cupid's strongest bow,

By his best arrow, with the golden head,

By the simplicity of Venus' doves,

By that which knitteth souls and prospers loves,

And by that fire which burn'd the Carthage queen,

When the false Trojan under sail was seen,—

By all the vows that ever men have broke,

In number more than ever women spoke,—

In that same place thou hast appointed me,

Tomorrow truly will I meet with thee.

LYSANDER

Keep promise, love. Look, here comes Helena.

[Enter HELENA.]

HERMIA

God speed fair Helena! Whither away?

HELENA

Call you me fair? that fair again unsay.

Demetrius loves your fair. O happy fair!

Your eyes are lode-stars; and your tongue's sweet air

More tuneable than lark to shepherd's ear,

When wheat is green, when hawthorn buds appear.

Sickness is catching: O, were favour so,

Yours would I catch, fair Hermia, ere I go;

My ear should catch your voice, my eye your eye,

My tongue should catch your tongue's sweet melody.

Were the world mine, Demetrius being bated,

The rest I'd give to be to you translated.

O, teach me how you look; and with what art

You sway the motion of Demetrius' heart!

HERMIA

I frown upon him, yet he loves me still.

HELENA

O that your frowns would teach my smiles such skill!

HERMIA

I give him curses, yet he gives me love.

HELENA

O that my prayers could such affection move!

HERMIA

The more I hate, the more he follows me.

HELENA

The more I love, the more he hateth me.

HERMIA

His folly, Helena, is no fault of mine.

HELENA

None, but your beauty: would that fault were mine!

HERMIA

Take comfort; he no more shall see my face;

Lysander and myself will fly this place.—

Before the time I did Lysander see,

Seem'd Athens as a paradise to me:

O, then, what graces in my love do dwell,

That he hath turn'd a heaven unto hell!

LYSANDER

Helen, to you our minds we will unfold:

To-morrow night, when Phoebe doth behold

Her silver visage in the watery glass,

Decking with liquid pearl the bladed grass,—

A time that lovers' flights doth still conceal,—

Through Athens' gates have we devis'd to steal.

HERMIA

And in the wood where often you and I

Upon faint primrose beds were wont to lie,

Emptying our bosoms of their counsel sweet,

There my Lysander and myself shall meet:

And thence from Athens turn away our eyes,

To seek new friends and stranger companies.

Farewell, sweet playfellow: pray thou for us,

And good luck grant thee thy Demetrius!—

Keep word, Lysander: we must starve our sight

From lovers' food, till morrow deep midnight.

LYSANDER

I will, my Hermia.

[Exit HERMIA.]

  Helena, adieu:

As you on him, Demetrius dote on you!

[Exit LYSANDER.]

HELENA

How happy some o'er other some can be!

Through Athens I am thought as fair as she.

But what of that? Demetrius thinks not so;

He will not know what all but he do know.

And as he errs, doting on Hermia's eyes,

So I, admiring of his qualities.

Things base and vile, holding no quantity,

Love can transpose to form and dignity.

Love looks not with the eyes, but with the mind;

And therefore is wing'd Cupid painted blind.

Nor hath love's mind of any judgment taste;

Wings and no eyes figure unheedy haste:

And therefore is love said to be a child,

Because in choice he is so oft beguil'd.

As waggish boys in game themselves forswear,

So the boy Love is perjur'd everywhere:

For ere Demetrius look'd on Hermia's eyne,

He hail'd down oaths that he was only mine;

And when this hail some heat from Hermia felt,

So he dissolv'd, and showers of oaths did melt.

I will go tell him of fair Hermia's flight;

Then to the wood will he to-morrow night

Pursue her; and for this intelligence

If I have thanks, it is a dear expense:

But herein mean I to enrich my pain,

To have his sight thither and back again.

[Exit HELENA.]

SCENE II. The Same. A Room in a Cottage

[Enter SNUG, BOTTOM, FLUTE, SNOUT, QUINCE, and STARVELING.]

QUINCE

Is all our company here?

BOTTOM

You were best to call them generally, man by man, according to the scrip.

QUINCE

Here is the scroll of every man's name, which is thought fit, through all Athens, to play in our interlude before the duke and duchess on his wedding-day at night.

BOTTOM

First, good Peter Quince, say what the play treats on; then read the names of the actors; and so grow to a point.

QUINCE

Marry, our play is—*The most lamentable comedy and most cruel death of Pyramus and Thisby.*

BOTTOM

A very good piece of work, I assure you, and a merry.— Now, good Peter Quince, call forth your actors by the scroll.— Masters, spread yourselves.

QUINCE

Answer, as I call you.—Nick Bottom, the weaver.

BOTTOM

Ready. Name what part I am for, and proceed.

QUINCE

You, Nick Bottom, are set down for Pyramus.

BOTTOM

What is Pyramus? a lover, or a tyrant?

QUINCE

A lover, that kills himself most gallantly for love.

BOTTOM

That will ask some tears in the true performing of it. If I do it, let the audience look to their eyes; I will move storms; I will condole in some measure. To the rest:—yet my chief humour is for a tyrant: I could play Ercles rarely, or a part to tear a cat in, to make all split.

The raging rocks

And shivering shocks

Shall break the locks

Of prison gates:

And Phibbus' car

Shall shine from far,

And make and mar

The foolish Fates.

This was lofty.—Now name the rest of the players.—This is Ercles' vein, a tyrant's vein;—a lover is more condoling.

QUINCE

Francis Flute, the bellows-mender.

FLUTE

Here, Peter Quince.

QUINCE

Flute, you must take Thisby on you.

FLUTE

What is Thisby? a wandering knight?

QUINCE

It is the lady that Pyramus must love.

FLUTE

Nay, faith, let not me play a woman; I have a beard coming.

QUINCE

That's all one; you shall play it in a mask, and you may speak as small as you will.

BOTTOM

An I may hide my face, let me play Thisby too: I'll speak in a monstrous little voice;—'Thisne, Thisne!'— 'Ah, Pyramus, my lover dear; thy Thisby dear! and lady dear!'

QUINCE

No, no, you must play Pyramus; and, Flute, you Thisby.

BOTTOM

Well, proceed.

QUINCE

Robin Starveling, the tailor.

STARVELING

Here, Peter Quince.

QUINCE

Robin Starveling, you must play Thisby's mother.—

Tom Snout, the tinker.

SNOUT

Here, Peter Quince.

QUINCE

You, Pyramus' father; myself, Thisby's father;—

Snug, the joiner, you, the lion's part:—and, I hope, here is a play fitted.

SNUG

Have you the lion's part written? pray you, if it be, give it me, for I am slow of study.

QUINCE

You may do it extempore, for it is nothing but roaring.

BOTTOM

Let me play the lion too: I will roar that I will do any man's heart good to hear me; I will roar that I will make the duke say 'Let him roar again, let him roar again.'

QUINCE

An you should do it too terribly, you would fright the duchess and the ladies, that they would shriek; and that were enough to hang us all.

ALL

That would hang us every mother's son.

BOTTOM

I grant you, friends, if you should fright the ladies out of their wits, they would have no more discretion but to hang us: but I will aggravate my voice so, that I will roar you as gently as any sucking dove; I will roar you an 'twere any nightingale.

QUINCE

You can play no part but Pyramus; for Pyramus is a sweet-faced man; a proper man, as one shall see in a summer's day; a most lovely gentleman-like man; therefore you must needs play Pyramus.

BOTTOM

Well, I will undertake it. What beard were I best to play it in?

QUINCE

Why, what you will.

BOTTOM

I will discharge it in either your straw-colour beard, your orange-tawny beard, your purple-in-grain beard, or your French-crown-colour beard, your perfect yellow.

QUINCE

Some of your French crowns have no hair at all, and then you will play bare-faced.— But, masters, here are your parts: and I am to entreat you, request you, and desire you, to con them by to-morrow night; and meet me in the palace wood, a mile without the town, by moonlight; there will we rehearse: for if we meet in the city, we shall be dogg'd with company, and our devices known. In the meantime I will draw a bill of properties, such as our play wants. I pray you, fail me not.

BOTTOM

We will meet; and there we may rehearse most obscenely and courageously. Take pains; be perfect; adieu.

QUINCE

At the duke's oak we meet.

BOTTOM

Enough; hold, or cut bow-strings.

[Exeunt.]

ACT II

SCENE I. A wood near Athens

[Enter a FAIRY at One door, and PUCK at another.]

PUCK

How now, spirit! whither wander you?

FAIRY

Over hill, over dale,

  Thorough bush, thorough brier,

Over park, over pale,

  Thorough flood, thorough fire,

I do wander everywhere,

Swifter than the moon's sphere;

And I serve the fairy queen,

To dew her orbs upon the green.

The cowslips tall her pensioners be:

In their gold coats spots you see;

Those be rubies, fairy favours,

In those freckles live their savours;

I must go seek some dew-drops here,

And hang a pearl in every cowslip's ear.

Farewell, thou lob of spirits; I'll be gone:

Our queen and all her elves come here anon.

PUCK

The king doth keep his revels here to-night;

Take heed the Queen come not within his sight.

For Oberon is passing fell and wrath,

Because that she, as her attendant, hath

A lovely boy, stol'n from an Indian king;

She never had so sweet a changeling:

And jealous Oberon would have the child

Knight of his train, to trace the forests wild:

But she perforce withholds the lovèd boy,

Crowns him with flowers, and makes him all her joy:

And now they never meet in grove or green,

By fountain clear, or spangled starlight sheen,

But they do square; that all their elves for fear

Creep into acorn cups, and hide them there.

FAIRY

Either I mistake your shape and making quite,

Or else you are that shrewd and knavish sprite

Call'd Robin Goodfellow: are not you he

That frights the maidens of the villagery;

Skim milk, and sometimes labour in the quern,

And bootless make the breathless housewife churn;

And sometime make the drink to bear no barm;

Mislead night-wanderers, laughing at their harm?

Those that Hobgoblin call you, and sweet Puck,

You do their work, and they shall have good luck:

Are not you he?

PUCK

       Thou speak'st aright;

I am that merry wanderer of the night.

I jest to Oberon, and make him smile,

When I a fat and bean-fed horse beguile,

Neighing in likeness of a filly foal;

And sometime lurk I in a gossip's bowl,

In very likeness of a roasted crab;

And, when she drinks, against her lips I bob,

And on her withered dewlap pour the ale.

The wisest aunt, telling the saddest tale,

Sometime for three-foot stool mistaketh me;

Then slip I from her bum, down topples she,

And 'tailor' cries, and falls into a cough;

And then the whole quire hold their hips and loffe,

And waxen in their mirth, and neeze, and swear

A merrier hour was never wasted there.—

But room, fairy, here comes Oberon.

FAIRY

And here my mistress.—Would that he were gone!

[Enter OBERON at one door, with his Train, and TITANIA, at another, with hers.]

OBERON

Ill met by moonlight, proud Titania.

TITANIA

What, jealous Oberon! Fairies, skip hence;

I have forsworn his bed and company.

OBERON

Tarry, rash wanton: am not I thy lord?

TITANIA

Then I must be thy lady; but I know

When thou hast stol'n away from fairy-land,

And in the shape of Corin sat all day,

Playing on pipes of corn, and versing love

To amorous Phillida. Why art thou here,

Come from the farthest steep of India,

But that, forsooth, the bouncing Amazon,

Your buskin'd mistress and your warrior love,

To Theseus must be wedded; and you come

To give their bed joy and prosperity.

OBERON

How canst thou thus, for shame, Titania,

Glance at my credit with Hippolyta,

Knowing I know thy love to Theseus?

Didst not thou lead him through the glimmering night

From Perigenia, whom he ravish'd?

And make him with fair Aegle break his faith,

With Ariadne and Antiopa?

TITANIA

These are the forgeries of jealousy:

And never, since the middle summer's spring,

Met we on hill, in dale, forest, or mead,

By pavèd fountain, or by rushy brook,

Or on the beachèd margent of the sea,

To dance our ringlets to the whistling wind,

But with thy brawls thou hast disturb'd our sport.

Therefore the winds, piping to us in vain,

As in revenge, have suck'd up from the sea

Contagious fogs; which, falling in the land,

Hath every pelting river made so proud

That they have overborne their continents:

The ox hath therefore stretch'd his yoke in vain,

The ploughman lost his sweat; and the green corn

Hath rotted ere his youth attain'd a beard:

The fold stands empty in the drownèd field,

And crows are fatted with the murrion flock;

The nine men's morris is fill'd up with mud;

And the quaint mazes in the wanton green,

For lack of tread, are undistinguishable:

The human mortals want their winter here;

No night is now with hymn or carol blest:—

Therefore the moon, the governess of floods,

Pale in her anger, washes all the air,

That rheumatic diseases do abound:

And thorough this distemperature we see

The seasons alter: hoary-headed frosts

Fall in the fresh lap of the crimson rose;

And on old Hyem's thin and icy crown

An odorous chaplet of sweet summer buds

Is, as in mockery, set: the spring, the summer,

The childing autumn, angry winter, change

Their wonted liveries; and the maz'd world,

By their increase, now knows not which is which:

And this same progeny of evils comes

From our debate, from our dissension:

We are their parents and original.

OBERON

Do you amend it, then: it lies in you:

Why should Titania cross her Oberon?

I do but beg a little changeling boy

To be my henchman.

TITANIA

            Set your heart at rest;

The fairy-land buys not the child of me.

His mother was a vot'ress of my order:

And, in the spicèd Indian air, by night,

Full often hath she gossip'd by my side;

And sat with me on Neptune's yellow sands,

Marking the embarkèd traders on the flood;

When we have laugh'd to see the sails conceive,

And grow big-bellied with the wanton wind;

Which she, with pretty and with swimming gait

Following,—her womb then rich with my young squire,—

Would imitate; and sail upon the land,

To fetch me trifles, and return again,

As from a voyage, rich with merchandise.

But she, being mortal, of that boy did die;

And for her sake do I rear up her boy:

And for her sake I will not part with him.

OBERON

How long within this wood intend you stay?

TITANIA

Perchance till after Theseus' wedding-day.

If you will patiently dance in our round,

And see our moonlight revels, go with us;

If not, shun me, and I will spare your haunts.

OBERON

Give me that boy and I will go with thee.

TITANIA

Not for thy fairy kingdom. Fairies, away:

We shall chide downright if I longer stay.

[Exit TITANIA with her Train.]

OBERON

Well, go thy way: thou shalt not from this grove

Till I torment thee for this injury.—

My gentle Puck, come hither: thou remember'st

Since once I sat upon a promontory,

And heard a mermaid, on a dolphin's back,

Uttering such dulcet and harmonious breath,

That the rude sea grew civil at her song,

And certain stars shot madly from their spheres

To hear the sea-maid's music.

PUCK

I remember.

OBERON

That very time I saw,—but thou couldst not,—

Flying between the cold moon and the earth,

Cupid, all arm'd: a certain aim he took

At a fair vestal, thronèd by the west;

And loos'd his love-shaft smartly from his bow,

As it should pierce a hundred thousand hearts;

But I might see young Cupid's fiery shaft

Quench'd in the chaste beams of the watery moon;

And the imperial votaress passed on,

In maiden meditation, fancy-free.

Yet mark'd I where the bolt of Cupid fell:

It fell upon a little western flower,—

Before milk-white, now purple with love's wound,—

And maidens call it love-in-idleness.

Fetch me that flower, the herb I showed thee once:

The juice of it on sleeping eyelids laid

Will make or man or woman madly dote

Upon the next live creature that it sees.

Fetch me this herb: and be thou here again

Ere the leviathan can swim a league.

PUCK

I'll put a girdle round about the earth

In forty minutes.

[Exit PUCK.]

OBERON

        Having once this juice,

I'll watch Titania when she is asleep,

And drop the liquor of it in her eyes:

The next thing then she waking looks upon,—

Be it on lion, bear, or wolf, or bull,

On meddling monkey, or on busy ape,—

She shall pursue it with the soul of love.

And ere I take this charm from off her sight,—

As I can take it with another herb,

I'll make her render up her page to me.

But who comes here? I am invisible;

And I will overhear their conference.

[Enter DEMETRIUS, HELENA following him.]

DEMETRIUS

I love thee not, therefore pursue me not.

Where is Lysander and fair Hermia?

The one I'll slay, the other slayeth me.

Thou told'st me they were stol'n into this wood,

And here am I, and wode within this wood,

Because I cannot meet with Hermia.

Hence, get thee gone, and follow me no more.

HELENA

You draw me, you hard-hearted adamant;

But yet you draw not iron, for my heart

Is true as steel. Leave you your power to draw,

And I shall have no power to follow you.

DEMETRIUS

Do I entice you? Do I speak you fair?

Or, rather, do I not in plainest truth

Tell you I do not, nor I cannot love you?

HELENA

And even for that do I love you the more.

I am your spaniel; and, Demetrius,

The more you beat me, I will fawn on you:

Use me but as your spaniel, spurn me, strike me,

Neglect me, lose me; only give me leave,

Unworthy as I am, to follow you.

What worser place can I beg in your love,

And yet a place of high respect with me,—

Than to be usèd as you use your dog?

DEMETRIUS

Tempt not too much the hatred of my spirit;

For I am sick when I do look on thee.

HELENA

And I am sick when I look not on you.

DEMETRIUS

You do impeach your modesty too much,

To leave the city, and commit yourself

Into the hands of one that loves you not;

To trust the opportunity of night,

And the ill counsel of a desert place,

With the rich worth of your virginity.

HELENA

Your virtue is my privilege for that.

It is not night when I do see your face,

Therefore I think I am not in the night;

Nor doth this wood lack worlds of company;

For you, in my respect, are all the world:

Then how can it be said I am alone

When all the world is here to look on me?

DEMETRIUS

I'll run from thee, and hide me in the brakes,

And leave thee to the mercy of wild beasts.

HELENA

The wildest hath not such a heart as you.

Run when you will, the story shall be chang'd;

Apollo flies, and Daphne holds the chase;

The dove pursues the griffin; the mild hind

Makes speed to catch the tiger,—bootless speed,

When cowardice pursues and valour flies.

DEMETRIUS

I will not stay thy questions; let me go:

Or, if thou follow me, do not believe

But I shall do thee mischief in the wood.

HELENA

Ay, in the temple, in the town, the field,

You do me mischief. Fie, Demetrius!

Your wrongs do set a scandal on my sex:

We cannot fight for love as men may do:

We should be woo'd, and were not made to woo.

I'll follow thee, and make a heaven of hell,

To die upon the hand I love so well.

[Exeunt DEMETRIUS and HELENA.]

OBERON

Fare thee well, nymph: ere he do leave this grove,

Thou shalt fly him, and he shall seek thy love.—

[Re-enter PUCK.]

Hast thou the flower there? Welcome, wanderer.

PUCK

Ay, there it is.

OBERON

       I pray thee give it me.

I know a bank whereon the wild thyme blows,

Where ox-lips and the nodding violet grows;

Quite over-canopied with luscious woodbine,

With sweet musk-roses, and with eglantine:

There sleeps Titania sometime of the night,

Lulled in these flowers with dances and delight;

And there the snake throws her enamell'd skin,

Weed wide enough to wrap a fairy in:

And with the juice of this I'll streak her eyes,

And make her full of hateful fantasies.

Take thou some of it, and seek through this grove:

A sweet Athenian lady is in love

With a disdainful youth: anoint his eyes;

But do it when the next thing he espies

May be the lady: thou shalt know the man

By the Athenian garments he hath on.

Effect it with some care, that he may prove

More fond on her than she upon her love:

And look thou meet me ere the first cock crow.

PUCK

Fear not, my lord; your servant shall do so.

[Exeunt.]

SCENE II.   Another part of the wood

[Enter TITANIA, with her Train.]

TITANIA

Come, now a roundel and a fairy song;

Then, for the third part of a minute, hence;

Some to kill cankers in the musk-rose buds;

Some war with rere-mice for their leathern wings,

To make my small elves coats; and some keep back

The clamorous owl, that nightly hoots and wonders

At our quaint spirits. Sing me now asleep;

Then to your offices, and let me rest.

SONG I

FIRST FAIRY

  You spotted snakes, with double tongue,

    Thorny hedgehogs, be not seen;

  Newts and blind-worms do no wrong;

    Come not near our fairy queen:

CHORUS.

  Philomel, with melody,

  Sing in our sweet lullaby:

Lulla, lulla, lullaby; lulla, lulla, lullaby:

  Never harm, nor spell, nor charm,

  Come our lovely lady nigh;

  So good-night, with lullaby.

SONG II

SECOND FAIRY

  Weaving spiders, come not here;

    Hence, you long-legg'd spinners, hence;

Beetles black, approach not near;

    Worm nor snail do no offence.

CHORUS

    Philomel with melody, &c.

FIRST FAIRY

Hence away; now all is well.

One, aloof, stand sentinel.

[Exeunt Fairies. TITANIA sleeps.]

[Enter OBERON.]

OBERON

What thou seest when thou dost wake,

[Squeezes the flower on TITANIA'S eyelids.]

Do it for thy true-love take;

Love and languish for his sake;

Be it ounce, or cat, or bear,

Pard, or boar with bristled hair,

In thy eye that shall appear

When thou wak'st, it is thy dear;

Wake when some vile thing is near.

[Exit.]

[Enter LYSANDER and HERMIA.]

LYSANDER

Fair love, you faint with wandering in the wood;

  And, to speak troth, I have forgot our way;

We'll rest us, Hermia, if you think it good,

  And tarry for the comfort of the day.

HERMIA

Be it so, Lysander: find you out a bed,

For I upon this bank will rest my head.

LYSANDER

One turf shall serve as pillow for us both;

One heart, one bed, two bosoms, and one troth.

HERMIA

Nay, good Lysander; for my sake, my dear,

Lie farther off yet, do not lie so near.

LYSANDER

O, take the sense, sweet, of my innocence;

Love takes the meaning in love's conference.

I mean that my heart unto yours is knit;

So that but one heart we can make of it:

Two bosoms interchainèd with an oath;

So then two bosoms and a single troth.

Then by your side no bed-room me deny;

For lying so, Hermia, I do not lie.

HERMIA

Lysander riddles very prettily:—

Now much beshrew my manners and my pride

If Hermia meant to say Lysander lied!

But, gentle friend, for love and courtesy

Lie further off; in human modesty,

Such separation as may well be said

Becomes a virtuous bachelor and a maid:

So far be distant; and good night, sweet friend:

Thy love ne'er alter till thy sweet life end!

LYSANDER

Amen, amen, to that fair prayer say I;

And then end life when I end loyalty!

Here is my bed: Sleep give thee all his rest!

HERMIA

With half that wish the wisher's eyes be pressed!

[They sleep.]

[Enter PUCK.]

PUCK

Through the forest have I gone,

But Athenian found I none,

On whose eyes I might approve

This flower's force in stirring love.

Night and silence! Who is here?

Weeds of Athens he doth wear:

This is he, my master said,

Despisèd the Athenian maid;

And here the maiden, sleeping sound,

On the dank and dirty ground.

Pretty soul! she durst not lie

Near this lack-love, this kill-courtesy.

Churl, upon thy eyes I throw

All the power this charm doth owe;

When thou wak'st let love forbid

Sleep his seat on thy eyelid:

So awake when I am gone;

For I must now to Oberon.

[Exit.]

[Enter DEMETRIUS and HELENA, running.]

HELENA

Stay, though thou kill me, sweet Demetrius.

DEMETRIUS

I charge thee, hence, and do not haunt me thus.

HELENA

O, wilt thou darkling leave me? do not so.

DEMETRIUS.

Stay on thy peril; I alone will go.

[Exit DEMETRIUS.]

HELENA

O, I am out of breath in this fond chase!

The more my prayer, the lesser is my grace.

Happy is Hermia, wheresoe'er she lies,

For she hath blessèd and attractive eyes.

How came her eyes so bright? Not with salt tears:

If so, my eyes are oftener wash'd than hers.

No, no, I am as ugly as a bear;

For beasts that meet me run away for fear:

Therefore no marvel though Demetrius

Do, as a monster, fly my presence thus.

What wicked and dissembling glass of mine

Made me compare with Hermia's sphery eyne?—

But who is here?—Lysander! on the ground!

Dead? or asleep? I see no blood, no wound.

Lysander, if you live, good sir, awake.

LYSANDER

[Waking.]

And run through fire I will for thy sweet sake.

Transparent Helena! Nature shows art,

That through thy bosom makes me see thy heart.

Where is Demetrius? O, how fit a word

Is that vile name to perish on my sword!

HELENA

Do not say so, Lysander; say not so:

What though he love your Hermia? Lord, what though?

Yet Hermia still loves you: then be content.

LYSANDER.

Content with Hermia? No: I do repent

The tedious minutes I with her have spent.

Not Hermia but Helena I love:

Who will not change a raven for a dove?

The will of man is by his reason sway'd;

And reason says you are the worthier maid.

Things growing are not ripe until their season;

So I, being young, till now ripe not to reason;

And touching now the point of human skill,

Reason becomes the marshal to my will,

And leads me to your eyes, where I o'erlook

Love's stories, written in love's richest book.

HELENA

Wherefore was I to this keen mockery born?

When at your hands did I deserve this scorn?

Is't not enough, is't not enough, young man,

That I did never, no, nor never can

Deserve a sweet look from Demetrius' eye,

But you must flout my insufficiency?

Good troth, you do me wrong,—good sooth, you do—

In such disdainful manner me to woo.

But fare you well: perforce I must confess,

I thought you lord of more true gentleness.

O, that a lady of one man refus'd

Should of another therefore be abus'd!

[Exit.]

LYSANDER

She sees not Hermia:—Hermia, sleep thou there;

And never mayst thou come Lysander near!

For, as a surfeit of the sweetest things

The deepest loathing to the stomach brings;

Or, as the heresies that men do leave

Are hated most of those they did deceive;

So thou, my surfeit and my heresy,

Of all be hated, but the most of me!

And, all my powers, address your love and might

To honour Helen, and to be her knight!

[Exit.]

HERMIA

[Starting.]

Help me, Lysander, help me! do thy best

To pluck this crawling serpent from my breast!

Ay me, for pity!—What a dream was here!

Lysander, look how I do quake with fear!

Methought a serpent eat my heart away,

And you sat smiling at his cruel prey.—

Lysander! what, removed? Lysander! lord!

What, out of hearing? gone? no sound, no word?

Alack, where are you? speak, an if you hear;

Speak, of all loves! I swoon almost with fear.

No?—then I well perceive you are not nigh:

Either death or you I'll find immediately.

[Exit.]

ACT III

SCENE I. The Wood. The Queen of Fairies lying asleep

[Enter QUINCE, SNUG, BOTTOM, FLUTE, SNOUT, and STARVELING.]

BOTTOM

Are we all met?

QUINCE

Pat, pat; and here's a marvellous convenient place for our rehearsal. This green plot shall be our stage, this hawthorn brake our tiring-house; and we will do it in action, as we will do it before the duke.

BOTTOM

Peter Quince,—

QUINCE

What sayest thou, bully Bottom?

BOTTOM

There are things in this comedy of 'Pyramus and Thisby' that will never please. First, Pyramus must draw a sword to kill himself; which the ladies cannot abide. How answer you that?

SNOUT

By'r lakin, a parlous fear.

STARVELING

I believe we must leave the killing out, when all is done.

BOTTOM

Not a whit: I have a device to make all well. Write me a prologue; and let the prologue seem to say we will do no harm with our swords, and that Pyramus is not killed indeed; and for the more better assurance, tell them that I Pyramus am not Pyramus but Bottom the weaver: this will put them out of fear.

QUINCE

Well, we will have such a prologue; and it shall be written in eight and six.

BOTTOM

No, make it two more; let it be written in eight and eight.

SNOUT

Will not the ladies be afeard of the lion?

STARVELING

I fear it, I promise you.

BOTTOM

Masters, you ought to consider with yourselves: to bring in, God shield us! a lion among ladies is a most dreadful thing: for there is not a more fearful wild-fowl than your lion living; and we ought to look to it.

SNOUT

Therefore another prologue must tell he is not a lion.

BOTTOM

Nay, you must name his name, and half his face must be seen through the lion's neck; and he himself must speak through, saying thus, or to the same defect,—'Ladies,' or, 'Fair ladies, I would wish you, or, I would request you, or, I would entreat you, not to fear, not to tremble:

my life for yours. If you think I come hither as a lion, it were pity of my life. No, I am no such thing; I am a man as other men are:'—and there, indeed, let him name his name, and tell them plainly he is Snug the joiner.

QUINCE

Well, it shall be so. But there is two hard things; that is, to bring the moonlight into a chamber: for, you know, Pyramus and Thisbe meet by moonlight.

SNOUT

Doth the moon shine that night we play our play?

BOTTOM

A calendar, a calendar! look in the almanack; find out moonshine, find out moonshine.

QUINCE

Yes, it doth shine that night.

BOTTOM

Why, then may you leave a casement of the great chamber-window, where we play, open; and the moon may shine in at the casement.

QUINCE

Ay; or else one must come in with a bush of thorns and a lantern, and say he comes to disfigure or to present the person of moonshine. Then there is another thing: we must have a wall in the great chamber; for Pyramus and Thisby, says the story, did talk through the chink of a wall.

SNOUT

You can never bring in a wall.—What say you, Bottom?

BOTTOM

Some man or other must present wall: and let him have some plaster, or some loam, or some rough-cast about him, to signify wall; and let him hold his fingers thus, and through that cranny shall Pyramus and Thisby whisper.

QUINCE

If that may be, then all is well. Come, sit down, every mother's son, and rehearse your parts. Pyramus, you begin: when you have spoken your speech, enter into that brake; and so every one according to his cue.

[Enter PUCK behind.]

PUCK

What hempen homespuns have we swaggering here,

So near the cradle of the fairy queen?

What, a play toward! I'll be an auditor;

An actor too perhaps, if I see cause.

QUINCE

Speak, Pyramus.—Thisby, stand forth.

PYRAMUS

'Thisby, the flowers of odious savours sweet,'

QUINCE

Odours, odours.

PYRAMUS

'—odours savours sweet:

So hath thy breath, my dearest Thisby dear.—

But hark, a voice! stay thou but here awhile,

And by and by I will to thee appear.'

[Exit.]

PUCK

A stranger Pyramus than e'er played here!

[Aside.—Exit.]

THISBE

Must I speak now?

QUINCE

Ay, marry, must you: for you must understand he goes but to see a noise that he heard, and is to come again.

THISBE

'Most radiant Pyramus, most lily white of hue,

Of colour like the red rose on triumphant brier,

Most brisky juvenal, and eke most lovely Jew,

As true as truest horse, that would never tire,

I'll meet thee, Pyramus, at Ninny's tomb.'

QUINCE

Ninus' tomb, man: why, you must not speak that yet: that you answer to Pyramus. You speak all your part at once, cues, and all.—Pyramus enter: your cue is past; it is 'never tire.'

THISBE

O,—'As true as truest horse, that yet would never tire.'

[Re-enter PUCK, and BOTTOM with an ass's head.]

PYRAMUS

'If I were fair, Thisby, I were only thine:—'

QUINCE

O monstrous! O strange! we are haunted. Pray, masters! fly, masters! Help!

[Exeunt Clowns.]

PUCK

I'll follow you; I'll lead you about a round,

Through bog, through bush, through brake, through brier;

Sometime a horse I'll be, sometime a hound,

A hog, a headless bear, sometime a fire;

And neigh, and bark, and grunt, and roar, and burn,

Like horse, hound, hog, bear, fire, at every turn.

[Exit.]

BOTTOM

Why do they run away? This is a knavery of them to make me afeard.

[Re-enter SNOUT.]

SNOUT

O Bottom, thou art changed! What do I see on thee?

BOTTOM

What do you see? you see an ass-head of your own, do you?

[Re-enter QUINCE.]

QUINCE

Bless thee, Bottom! bless thee! thou art translated.

[Exit.]

BOTTOM

I see their knavery: this is to make an ass of me; to fright me, if they could. But I will not stir from this place, do what they can: I will walk up and down here, and I will sing, that they shall hear I am not afraid.

[Sings.]

    The ousel cock, so black of hue,

        With orange-tawny bill,

    The throstle with his note so true,

        The wren with little quill.

TITANIA

[Waking.]

What angel wakes me from my flowery bed?

BOTTOM

[Sings.]

    The finch, the sparrow, and the lark,

        The plain-song cuckoo gray,

    Whose note full many a man doth mark,

And dares not answer nay;—

for, indeed, who would set his wit to so foolish a bird? Who would give a bird the lie, though he cry 'cuckoo' never so?

TITANIA

I pray thee, gentle mortal, sing again;

Mine ear is much enamour'd of thy note.

So is mine eye enthrallèd to thy shape;

And thy fair virtue's force perforce doth move me,

On the first view, to say, to swear, I love thee.

BOTTOM

Methinks, mistress, you should have little reason for that: and yet, to say the truth, reason and love keep little company together now-a-days: the more the pity that some honest neighbours will not make them friends. Nay, I can gleek upon occasion.

TITANIA

Thou art as wise as thou art beautiful.

BOTTOM

Not so, neither: but if I had wit enough to get out of this wood, I have enough to serve mine own turn.

TITANIA

Out of this wood do not desire to go;

Thou shalt remain here whether thou wilt or no.

I am a spirit of no common rate,—

The summer still doth tend upon my state;

And I do love thee: therefore, go with me,

I'll give thee fairies to attend on thee;

And they shall fetch thee jewels from the deep,

And sing, while thou on pressèd flowers dost sleep:

And I will purge thy mortal grossness so

That thou shalt like an airy spirit go.—

Peasblossom! Cobweb! Moth! and Mustardseed!

[Enter Four Fairies.]

FIRST FAIRY

Ready.

SECOND FAIRY

And I.

THIRD FAIRY

And I.

FOURTH FAIRY

Where shall we go?

TITANIA

Be kind and courteous to this gentleman;

Hop in his walks and gambol in his eyes;

Feed him with apricocks and dewberries,

With purple grapes, green figs, and mulberries;

The honey bags steal from the humble-bees,

And, for night-tapers, crop their waxen thighs,

And light them at the fiery glow-worm's eyes,

To have my love to bed and to arise;

And pluck the wings from painted butterflies,

To fan the moonbeams from his sleeping eyes:

Nod to him, elves, and do him courtesies.

FIRST FAIRY

Hail, mortal!

SECOND FAIRY

Hail!

THIRD FAIRY

Hail!

FOURTH FAIRY

Hail!

BOTTOM

I cry your worships mercy, heartily.—I beseech your worship's name.

COBWEB

Cobweb.

BOTTOM

I shall desire you of more acquaintance, good Master Cobweb. If I cut my finger, I shall make bold with you.—Your name, honest gentleman?

PEASBLOSSOM

Peasblossom.

BOTTOM

I pray you, commend me to Mistress Squash, your mother, and to Master Peascod, your father. Good Master Peasblossom, I shall desire you of more acquaintance too.—Your name, I beseech you, sir?

MUSTARDSEED

Mustardseed.

BOTTOM

Good Master Mustardseed, I know your patience well: That same cowardly giant-like ox-beef hath devoured many a gentleman of your house: I promise you your kindred hath made my eyes water ere now. I desire you of more acquaintance, good Master Mustardseed.

TITANIA

Come, wait upon him; lead him to my bower.

The moon, methinks, looks with a watery eye;

And when she weeps, weeps every little flower;

Lamenting some enforced chastity.

Tie up my love's tongue, bring him silently.

[Exeunt.]

SCENE II.   Another part of the wood

[Enter OBERON.]

OBERON

I wonder if Titania be awak'd;

Then, what it was that next came in her eye,

Which she must dote on in extremity.

[Enter PUCK.]

Here comes my messenger.—How now, mad spirit?

What night-rule now about this haunted grove?

PUCK

My mistress with a monster is in love.

Near to her close and consecrated bower,

While she was in her dull and sleeping hour,

A crew of patches, rude mechanicals,

That work for bread upon Athenian stalls,

Were met together to rehearse a play

Intended for great Theseus' nuptial day.

The shallowest thickskin of that barren sort

Who Pyramus presented in their sport,

Forsook his scene and enter'd in a brake;

When I did him at this advantage take,

An ass's nowl I fixed on his head;

Anon, his Thisbe must be answerèd,

And forth my mimic comes. When they him spy,

As wild geese that the creeping fowler eye,

Or russet-pated choughs, many in sort,

Rising and cawing at the gun's report,

Sever themselves and madly sweep the sky,

So at his sight away his fellows fly:

And at our stamp here, o'er and o'er one falls;

He murder cries, and help from Athens calls.

Their sense thus weak, lost with their fears, thus strong,

Made senseless things begin to do them wrong;

For briers and thorns at their apparel snatch;

Some sleeves, some hats: from yielders all things catch.

I led them on in this distracted fear,

And left sweet Pyramus translated there:

When in that moment,—so it came to pass,—

Titania wak'd, and straightway lov'd an ass.

OBERON

This falls out better than I could devise.

But hast thou yet latch'd the Athenian's eyes

With the love-juice, as I did bid thee do?

PUCK

I took him sleeping,—that is finish'd too,—

And the Athenian woman by his side;

That, when he wak'd, of force she must be ey'd.

[Enter DEMETRIUS and HERMIA.]

OBERON

Stand close; this is the same Athenian.

PUCK

This is the woman, but not this the man.

DEMETRIUS

O, why rebuke you him that loves you so?

Lay breath so bitter on your bitter foe.

HERMIA

Now I but chide, but I should use thee worse;

For thou, I fear, hast given me cause to curse.

If thou hast slain Lysander in his sleep,

Being o'er shoes in blood, plunge in the deep,

And kill me too.

The sun was not so true unto the day

As he to me: would he have stol'n away

From sleeping Hermia? I'll believe as soon

This whole earth may be bor'd; and that the moon

May through the centre creep and so displease

Her brother's noontide with the antipodes.

It cannot be but thou hast murder'd him;

So should a murderer look; so dead, so grim.

DEMETRIUS

So should the murder'd look; and so should I,

Pierc'd through the heart with your stern cruelty:

Yet you, the murderer, look as bright, as clear,

As yonder Venus in her glimmering sphere.

HERMIA

What's this to my Lysander? where is he?

Ah, good Demetrius, wilt thou give him me?

DEMETRIUS

I had rather give his carcass to my hounds.

HERMIA

Out, dog! out, cur! thou driv'st me past the bounds

Of maiden's patience. Hast thou slain him, then?

Henceforth be never number'd among men!

Oh! once tell true; tell true, even for my sake;

Durst thou have look'd upon him, being awake,

And hast thou kill'd him sleeping? O brave touch!

Could not a worm, an adder, do so much?

An adder did it; for with doubler tongue

Than thine, thou serpent, never adder stung.

DEMETRIUS

You spend your passion on a mispris'd mood:

I am not guilty of Lysander's blood;

Nor is he dead, for aught that I can tell.

HERMIA

I pray thee, tell me, then, that he is well.

DEMETRIUS

An if I could, what should I get therefore?

HERMIA

A privilege never to see me more.—

And from thy hated presence part I so:

See me no more whether he be dead or no.

[Exit.]

DEMETRIUS

There is no following her in this fierce vein:

Here, therefore, for a while I will remain.

So sorrow's heaviness doth heavier grow

For debt that bankrupt sleep doth sorrow owe;

Which now in some slight measure it will pay,

If for his tender here I make some stay.

[Lies down.]

OBERON

What hast thou done? thou hast mistaken quite,

And laid the love-juice on some true-love's sight:

Of thy misprision must perforce ensue

Some true love turn'd, and not a false turn'd true.

PUCK

Then fate o'er-rules, that, one man holding troth,

A million fail, confounding oath on oath.

OBERON

About the wood go, swifter than the wind,

And Helena of Athens look thou find:

All fancy-sick she is, and pale of cheer,

With sighs of love, that costs the fresh blood dear.

By some illusion see thou bring her here;

I'll charm his eyes against she do appear.

PUCK

I go, I go; look how I go,—

Swifter than arrow from the Tartar's bow.

[Exit.]

OBERON

  Flower of this purple dye,

  Hit with Cupid's archery,

  Sink in apple of his eye!

  When his love he doth espy,

  Let her shine as gloriously

As the Venus of the sky.—

When thou wak'st, if she be by,

Beg of her for remedy.

[Re-enter PUCK.]

PUCK

Captain of our fairy band,

Helena is here at hand,

And the youth mistook by me

Pleading for a lover's fee;

Shall we their fond pageant see?

Lord, what fools these mortals be!

OBERON

Stand aside: the noise they make

Will cause Demetrius to awake.

PUCK

Then will two at once woo one,—

That must needs be sport alone;

And those things do best please me

That befall preposterously.

[Enter LYSANDER and HELENA.]

LYSANDER

Why should you think that I should woo in scorn?

Scorn and derision never come in tears.

Look when I vow, I weep; and vows so born,

  In their nativity all truth appears.

How can these things in me seem scorn to you,

Bearing the badge of faith, to prove them true?

HELENA

You do advance your cunning more and more.

  When truth kills truth, O devilish-holy fray!

These vows are Hermia's: will you give her o'er?

  Weigh oath with oath, and you will nothing weigh:

Your vows to her and me, put in two scales,

Will even weigh; and both as light as tales.

LYSANDER

I had no judgment when to her I swore.

HELENA

Nor none, in my mind, now you give her o'er.

LYSANDER

Demetrius loves her, and he loves not you.

DEMETRIUS

[Awaking.]

O Helen, goddess, nymph, perfect, divine!

To what, my love, shall I compare thine eyne?

Crystal is muddy. O, how ripe in show

Thy lips, those kissing cherries, tempting grow!

That pure congealèd white, high Taurus' snow,

Fann'd with the eastern wind, turns to a crow

When thou hold'st up thy hand: O, let me kiss

This princess of pure white, this seal of bliss!

HELENA

O spite! O hell! I see you all are bent

To set against me for your merriment.

If you were civil, and knew courtesy,

You would not do me thus much injury.

Can you not hate me, as I know you do,

But you must join in souls to mock me too?

If you were men, as men you are in show,

You would not use a gentle lady so;

To vow, and swear, and superpraise my parts,

When I am sure you hate me with your hearts.

You both are rivals, and love Hermia;

And now both rivals, to mock Helena:

A trim exploit, a manly enterprise,

To conjure tears up in a poor maid's eyes

With your derision! None of noble sort

Would so offend a virgin, and extort

A poor soul's patience, all to make you sport.

LYSANDER

You are unkind, Demetrius; be not so;

For you love Hermia: this you know I know:

And here, with all good will, with all my heart,

In Hermia's love I yield you up my part;

And yours of Helena to me bequeath,

Whom I do love and will do till my death.

HELENA

Never did mockers waste more idle breath.

DEMETRIUS

Lysander, keep thy Hermia; I will none:

If e'er I lov'd her, all that love is gone.

My heart to her but as guest-wise sojourn'd;

And now to Helen is it home return'd,

There to remain.

LYSANDER

       Helen, it is not so.

DEMETRIUS

Disparage not the faith thou dost not know,

Lest, to thy peril, thou aby it dear.—

Look where thy love comes; yonder is thy dear.

[Enter HERMIA.]

HERMIA

Dark night, that from the eye his function takes,

The ear more quick of apprehension makes;

Wherein it doth impair the seeing sense,

It pays the hearing double recompense:—

Thou art not by mine eye, Lysander, found;

Mine ear, I thank it, brought me to thy sound.

But why unkindly didst thou leave me so?

LYSANDER

Why should he stay whom love doth press to go?

HERMIA

What love could press Lysander from my side?

LYSANDER

Lysander's love, that would not let him bide,—

Fair Helena,—who more engilds the night

Than all yon fiery oes and eyes of light.

Why seek'st thou me? could not this make thee know

The hate I bare thee made me leave thee so?

HERMIA

You speak not as you think; it cannot be.

HELENA

Lo, she is one of this confederacy!

Now I perceive they have conjoin'd all three

To fashion this false sport in spite of me.

Injurious Hermia! most ungrateful maid!

Have you conspir'd, have you with these contriv'd,

To bait me with this foul derision?

Is all the counsel that we two have shar'd,

The sisters' vows, the hours that we have spent,

When we have chid the hasty-footed time

For parting us,—O, is all forgot?

All school-days' friendship, childhood innocence?

We, Hermia, like two artificial gods,

Have with our needles created both one flower,

Both on one sampler, sitting on one cushion,

Both warbling of one song, both in one key;

As if our hands, our sides, voices, and minds,

Had been incorporate. So we grew together,

Like to a double cherry, seeming parted;

But yet a union in partition,

Two lovely berries moulded on one stem:

So, with two seeming bodies, but one heart;

Two of the first, like coats in heraldry,

Due but to one, and crownèd with one crest.

And will you rent our ancient love asunder,

To join with men in scorning your poor friend?

It is not friendly, 'tis not maidenly:

Our sex, as well as I, may chide you for it,

Though I alone do feel the injury.

HERMIA

I am amazèd at your passionate words:

I scorn you not; it seems that you scorn me.

HELENA

Have you not set Lysander, as in scorn,

To follow me, and praise my eyes and face?

And made your other love, Demetrius,—

Who even but now did spurn me with his foot,—

To call me goddess, nymph, divine, and rare,

Precious, celestial? Wherefore speaks he this

To her he hates? and wherefore doth Lysander

Deny your love, so rich within his soul,

And tender me, forsooth, affection,

But by your setting on, by your consent?

What though I be not so in grace as you,

So hung upon with love, so fortunate;

But miserable most, to love unlov'd?

This you should pity rather than despise.

HERMIA

I understand not what you mean by this.

HELENA

Ay, do persever, counterfeit sad looks,

Make mows upon me when I turn my back;

Wink each at other; hold the sweet jest up:

This sport, well carried, shall be chronicled.

If you have any pity, grace, or manners,

You would not make me such an argument.

But fare ye well: 'tis partly my own fault;

Which death, or absence, soon shall remedy.

LYSANDER

Stay, gentle Helena; hear my excuse;

My love, my life, my soul, fair Helena!

HELENA

O excellent!

HERMIA

    Sweet, do not scorn her so.

DEMETRIUS

If she cannot entreat, I can compel.

LYSANDER

Thou canst compel no more than she entreat;

Thy threats have no more strength than her weak prayers.—

Helen, I love thee; by my life I do;

I swear by that which I will lose for thee

To prove him false that says I love thee not.

DEMETRIUS

I say I love thee more than he can do.

LYSANDER

If thou say so, withdraw, and prove it too.

DEMETRIUS

Quick, come,—

HERMIA

           Lysander, whereto tends all this?

LYSANDER

Away, you Ethiope!

DEMETRIUS

           No, no, sir:—he will

Seem to break loose; take on as you would follow:

But yet come not. You are a tame man; go!

LYSANDER

Hang off, thou cat, thou burr: vile thing, let loose,

Or I will shake thee from me like a serpent.

HERMIA

Why are you grown so rude? what change is this,

Sweet love?

LYSANDER

       Thy love! out, tawny Tartar, out!

Out, loathèd medicine! hated potion, hence!

HERMIA

Do you not jest?

HELENA

       Yes, sooth; and so do you.

LYSANDER

Demetrius, I will keep my word with thee.

DEMETRIUS

I would I had your bond; for I perceive

A weak bond holds you; I'll not trust your word.

LYSANDER

What! should I hurt her, strike her, kill her dead?

Although I hate her, I'll not harm her so.

HERMIA

What! can you do me greater harm than hate?

Hate me! wherefore? O me! what news, my love?

Am not I Hermia? Are not you Lysander?

I am as fair now as I was erewhile.

Since night you lov'd me; yet since night you left me:

Why then, you left me,—O, the gods forbid!—

In earnest, shall I say?

LYSANDER

            Ay, by my life;

And never did desire to see thee more.

Therefore be out of hope, of question, doubt,

Be certain, nothing truer; 'tis no jest

That I do hate thee and love Helena.

HERMIA

O me! you juggler! you cankerblossom!

You thief of love! What! have you come by night,

And stol'n my love's heart from him?

HELENA

              Fine, i' faith!

Have you no modesty, no maiden shame,

No touch of bashfulness? What! will you tear

Impatient answers from my gentle tongue?

Fie, fie! you counterfeit, you puppet, you!

HERMIA

Puppet! why so? Ay, that way goes the game.

Now I perceive that she hath made compare

Between our statures; she hath urg'd her height;

And with her personage, her tall personage,

Her height, forsooth, she hath prevail'd with him.—

And are you grown so high in his esteem

Because I am so dwarfish and so low?

How low am I, thou painted maypole? speak;

How low am I? I am not yet so low

But that my nails can reach unto thine eyes.

HELENA

I pray you, though you mock me, gentlemen,

Let her not hurt me. I was never curst;

I have no gift at all in shrewishness;

I am a right maid for my cowardice;

Let her not strike me. You perhaps may think,

Because she is something lower than myself,

That I can match her.

HERMIA

Lower! hark, again.

HELENA

Good Hermia, do not be so bitter with me.

I evermore did love you, Hermia;

Did ever keep your counsels; never wrong'd you;

Save that, in love unto Demetrius,

I told him of your stealth unto this wood:

He follow'd you; for love I follow'd him;

But he hath chid me hence, and threaten'd me

To strike me, spurn me, nay, to kill me too:

And now, so you will let me quiet go,

To Athens will I bear my folly back,

And follow you no farther. Let me go:

You see how simple and how fond I am.

HERMIA

Why, get you gone: who is't that hinders you?

HELENA

A foolish heart that I leave here behind.

HERMIA

What! with Lysander?

HELENA

With Demetrius.

LYSANDER

Be not afraid; she shall not harm thee, Helena.

DEMETRIUS

No, sir, she shall not, though you take her part.

HELENA

O, when she's angry, she is keen and shrewd:

She was a vixen when she went to school;

And, though she be but little, she is fierce.

HERMIA

Little again! nothing but low and little!—

Why will you suffer her to flout me thus?

Let me come to her.

LYSANDER

Get you gone, you dwarf;

You minimus, of hind'ring knot-grass made;

You bead, you acorn.

DEMETRIUS

You are too officious

In her behalf that scorns your services.

Let her alone: speak not of Helena;

Take not her part; for if thou dost intend

Never so little show of love to her,

Thou shalt aby it.

LYSANDER

                Now she holds me not;

Now follow, if thou dar'st, to try whose right,

Of thine or mine, is most in Helena.

DEMETRIUS

Follow! nay, I'll go with thee, cheek by jole.

[Exeunt LYSANDER and DEMETRIUS.]

HERMIA

You, mistress, all this coil is 'long of you:

Nay, go not back.

HELENA

               I will not trust you, I;

Nor longer stay in your curst company.

Your hands than mine are quicker for a fray;

My legs are longer though, to run away.

[Exit.]

HERMIA

I am amaz'd, and know not what to say.

[Exit, pursuing HELENA.]

OBERON

This is thy negligence: still thou mistak'st,

Or else commit'st thy knaveries willfully.

PUCK

Believe me, king of shadows, I mistook.

Did not you tell me I should know the man

By the Athenian garments he had on?

And so far blameless proves my enterprise

That I have 'nointed an Athenian's eyes:

And so far am I glad it so did sort,

As this their jangling I esteem a sport.

OBERON

Thou seest these lovers seek a place to fight;

Hie therefore, Robin, overcast the night;

The starry welkin cover thou anon

With drooping fog, as black as Acheron,

And lead these testy rivals so astray

As one come not within another's way.

Like to Lysander sometime frame thy tongue,

Then stir Demetrius up with bitter wrong;

And sometime rail thou like Demetrius;

And from each other look thou lead them thus,

Till o'er their brows death-counterfeiting sleep

With leaden legs and batty wings doth creep:

Then crush this herb into Lysander's eye;

Whose liquor hath this virtuous property,

To take from thence all error with his might

And make his eyeballs roll with wonted sight.

When they next wake, all this derision

Shall seem a dream and fruitless vision;

And back to Athens shall the lovers wend

With league whose date till death shall never end.

Whiles I in this affair do thee employ,

I'll to my queen, and beg her Indian boy;

And then I will her charmèd eye release

From monster's view, and all things shall be peace.

PUCK

My fairy lord, this must be done with haste,

For night's swift dragons cut the clouds full fast;

And yonder shines Aurora's harbinger,

At whose approach ghosts, wandering here and there,

Troop home to churchyards: damnèd spirits all,

That in cross-ways and floods have burial,

Already to their wormy beds are gone;

For fear lest day should look their shames upon

They wilfully exile themselves from light,

And must for aye consort with black-brow'd night.

OBERON

But we are spirits of another sort:

I with the morning's love have oft made sport;

And, like a forester, the groves may tread

Even till the eastern gate, all fiery-red,

Opening on Neptune with fair blessèd beams,

Turns into yellow gold his salt-green streams.

But, notwithstanding, haste; make no delay:

We may effect this business yet ere day.

[Exit OBERON.]

PUCK

  Up and down, up and down;

  I will lead them up and down:

  I am fear'd in field and town.

  Goblin, lead them up and down.

Here comes one.

[Enter LYSANDER.]

LYSANDER

Where art thou, proud Demetrius? speak thou now.

PUCK

Here, villain; drawn and ready. Where art thou?

LYSANDER

I will be with thee straight.

PUCK

Follow me, then,

To plainer ground.

[Exit LYSANDER as following the voice.]

[Enter DEMETRIUS.]

DEMETRIUS

Lysander! speak again.

Thou runaway, thou coward, art thou fled?

Speak. In some bush? where dost thou hide thy head?

PUCK

Thou coward, art thou bragging to the stars,

Telling the bushes that thou look'st for wars,

And wilt not come? Come, recreant; come, thou child;

I'll whip thee with a rod: he is defiled

That draws a sword on thee.

DEMETRIUS

Yea, art thou there?

PUCK

Follow my voice; we'll try no manhood here.

[Exeunt.]

[Re-enter LYSANDER.]

LYSANDER

He goes before me, and still dares me on;

When I come where he calls, then he is gone.

The villain is much lighter heeled than I:

I follow'd fast, but faster he did fly;

That fallen am I in dark uneven way,

And here will rest me. Come, thou gentle day!

[Lies down.]

For if but once thou show me thy grey light,

I'll find Demetrius, and revenge this spite.

[Sleeps.]

[Re-enter PUCK and DEMETRIUS.]

PUCK

Ho, ho, ho, ho! Coward, why com'st thou not?

DEMETRIUS

Abide me, if thou dar'st; for well I wot

Thou runn'st before me, shifting every place;

And dar'st not stand, nor look me in the face.

Where art thou?

PUCK

        Come hither; I am here.

DEMETRIUS

Nay, then, thou mock'st me.

Thou shalt buy this dear,

If ever I thy face by daylight see:

Now, go thy way. Faintness constraineth me

To measure out my length on this cold bed.—

By day's approach look to be visited.

[Lies down and sleeps.]

[Enter HELENA.]

HELENA

O weary night, O long and tedious night,

   Abate thy hours! Shine comforts from the east,

That I may back to Athens by daylight,

   From these that my poor company detest:—

And sleep, that sometimes shuts up sorrow's eye,

Steal me awhile from mine own company.

[Sleeps.]

PUCK

   Yet but three? Come one more;

Two of both kinds makes up four.

Here she comes, curst and sad:—

Cupid is a knavish lad,

Thus to make poor females mad.

[Enter HERMIA.]

HERMIA

Never so weary, never so in woe,

  Bedabbled with the dew, and torn with briers;

I can no further crawl, no further go;

  My legs can keep no pace with my desires.

Here will I rest me till the break of day.

Heavens shield Lysander, if they mean a fray!

[Lies down.]

PUCK

    On the ground

    Sleep sound:

    I'll apply

    To your eye,

  Gentle lover, remedy.

[Squeezing the juice on LYSANDER'S eye.]

    When thou wak'st,

    Thou tak'st

True delight

In the sight

Of thy former lady's eye:

And the country proverb known,

That every man should take his own,

In your waking shall be shown:

Jack shall have Jill;

Nought shall go ill;

The man shall have his mare again, and all shall be well.

[Exit PUCK.—DEMETRIUS, HELENA &c, sleep.]

ACT IV

SCENE I. The Wood

[Enter TITANIA and BOTTOM; PEASBLOSSOM, COBWEB, MOTH, MUSTARDSEED, and other FAIRIES attending; OBERON behind, unseen.]

TITANIA

Come, sit thee down upon this flowery bed,

  While I thy amiable cheeks do coy,

And stick musk-roses in thy sleek smooth head,

  And kiss thy fair large ears, my gentle joy.

BOTTOM

Where's Peasblossom?

PEASBLOSSOM

Ready.

BOTTOM

Scratch my head, Peasblossom.— Where's Monsieur Cobweb?

COBWEB

Ready.

BOTTOM

Monsieur Cobweb; good monsieur, get you your weapons in your hand and kill me a red-hipped humble-bee on the top of a thistle; and, good monsieur, bring me the honey-bag. Do not fret yourself too much in the action, monsieur; and, good monsieur, have a care the honey-bag break not; I would be loath to have you overflown with a honey-bag, signior.— Where's Monsieur Mustardseed?

MUSTARDSEED

Ready.

BOTTOM

Give me your neif, Monsieur Mustardseed. Pray you, leave your curtsy, good monsieur.

MUSTARDSEED

What's your will?

BOTTOM

Nothing, good monsieur, but to help Cavalero Cobweb to scratch. I must to the barber's, monsieur; for methinks I am marvellous hairy about the face; and I am such a tender ass, if my hair do but tickle me I must scratch.

TITANIA

What, wilt thou hear some music, my sweet love?

BOTTOM

I have a reasonable good ear in music; let us have the tongs and the bones.

TITANIA

Or say, sweet love, what thou desirest to eat.

BOTTOM

Truly, a peck of provender; I could munch your good dry oats. Methinks I have a great desire to a bottle of hay: good hay, sweet hay, hath no fellow.

TITANIA

I have a venturous fairy that shall seek

The squirrel's hoard, and fetch thee new nuts.

BOTTOM

I had rather have a handful or two of dried peas. But, I pray you, let none of your people stir me; I have an exposition of sleep come upon me.

TITANIA

Sleep thou, and I will wind thee in my arms.

Fairies, be gone, and be all ways away.

So doth the woodbine the sweet honeysuckle

Gently entwist,—the female ivy so

Enrings the barky fingers of the elm.

O, how I love thee! how I dote on thee!

[They sleep.]

[OBERON advances. Enter PUCK.]

OBERON

Welcome, good Robin. Seest thou this sweet sight?

Her dotage now I do begin to pity.

For, meeting her of late behind the wood,

Seeking sweet favours for this hateful fool,

I did upbraid her and fall out with her:

For she his hairy temples then had rounded

With coronet of fresh and fragrant flowers;

And that same dew, which sometime on the buds

Was wont to swell like round and orient pearls,

Stood now within the pretty flow'rets' eyes,

Like tears that did their own disgrace bewail.

When I had, at my pleasure, taunted her,

And she, in mild terms, begg'd my patience,

I then did ask of her her changeling child;

Which straight she gave me, and her fairy sent

To bear him to my bower in fairy-land.

And now I have the boy, I will undo

This hateful imperfection of her eyes.

And, gentle Puck, take this transformèd scalp

From off the head of this Athenian swain,

That he awaking when the other do,

May all to Athens back again repair,

And think no more of this night's accidents

But as the fierce vexation of a dream.

But first I will release the fairy queen.

  Be as thou wast wont to be;

[Touching her eyes with an herb.]

  See as thou was wont to see.

Dian's bud o'er Cupid's flower

Hath such force and blessed power.

Now, my Titania; wake you, my sweet queen.

TITANIA

My Oberon! what visions have I seen!

Methought I was enamour'd of an ass.

OBERON

There lies your love.

TITANIA

               How came these things to pass?

O, how mine eyes do loathe his visage now!

OBERON

Silence awhile.—Robin, take off this head.

Titania, music call; and strike more dead

Than common sleep, of all these five, the sense.

TITANIA

Music, ho! music; such as charmeth sleep.

PUCK

Now when thou wak'st, with thine own fool's eyes peep.

OBERON

Sound, music.

[Still music.]

Come, my queen, take hands with me,

And rock the ground whereon these sleepers be.

Now thou and I are new in amity,

And will to-morrow midnight solemnly

Dance in Duke Theseus' house triumphantly,

And bless it to all fair prosperity:

There shall the pairs of faithful lovers be

Wedded, with Theseus, all in jollity.

PUCK

Fairy king, attend and mark;

I do hear the morning lark.

OBERON

Then, my queen, in silence sad,

Trip we after night's shade.

We the globe can compass soon,

Swifter than the wand'ring moon.

TITANIA

Come, my lord; and in our flight,

Tell me how it came this night

That I sleeping here was found

With these mortals on the ground.

[Exeunt. Horns sound within.]

[Enter THESEUS, HIPPOLYTA, EGEUS, and Train.]

THESEUS

Go, one of you, find out the forester;—

For now our observation is perform'd;

And since we have the vaward of the day,

My love shall hear the music of my hounds,—

Uncouple in the western valley; go:—

Despatch, I say, and find the forester.—

[Exit an ATTENDANT.]

We will, fair queen, up to the mountain's top,

And mark the musical confusion

Of hounds and echo in conjunction.

HIPPOLYTA

I was with Hercules and Cadmus once

When in a wood of Crete they bay'd the bear

With hounds of Sparta: never did I hear

Such gallant chiding; for, besides the groves,

The skies, the fountains, every region near

Seem'd all one mutual cry: I never heard

So musical a discord, such sweet thunder.

THESEUS

My hounds are bred out of the Spartan kind,

So flew'd, so sanded; and their heads are hung

With ears that sweep away the morning dew;

Crook-knee'd and dew-lap'd like Thessalian bulls;

Slow in pursuit, but match'd in mouth like bells,

Each under each. A cry more tuneable

Was never holla'd to, nor cheer'd with horn,

In Crete, in Sparta, nor in Thessaly.

Judge when you hear.—But, soft, what nymphs are these?

EGEUS

My lord, this is my daughter here asleep;

And this Lysander; this Demetrius is;

This Helena, old Nedar's Helena:

I wonder of their being here together.

THESEUS

No doubt they rose up early to observe

The rite of May; and, hearing our intent,

Came here in grace of our solemnity.—

But speak, Egeus; is not this the day

That Hermia should give answer of her choice?

EGEUS

It is, my lord.

THESEUS

Go, bid the huntsmen wake them with their horns.

[Horns, and shout within. DEMETRIUS, LYSANDER,HERMIA, and HELENA awake and start up.]

Good-morrow, friends. Saint Valentine is past;

Begin these wood-birds but to couple now?

LYSANDER

Pardon, my lord.

[He and the rest kneel to THESEUS.]

THESEUS

               I pray you all, stand up.

I know you two are rival enemies;

How comes this gentle concord in the world,

That hatred is so far from jealousy

To sleep by hate, and fear no enmity?

LYSANDER

My lord, I shall reply amazedly,

Half 'sleep, half waking; but as yet, I swear,

I cannot truly say how I came here:

But, as I think,—for truly would I speak—

And now I do bethink me, so it is,—

I came with Hermia hither: our intent

95

Was to be gone from Athens, where we might be,

Without the peril of the Athenian law.

EGEUS

Enough, enough, my lord; you have enough;

I beg the law, the law upon his head.—

They would have stol'n away, they would, Demetrius,

Thereby to have defeated you and me:

You of your wife, and me of my consent,—

Of my consent that she should be your wife.

DEMETRIUS

My lord, fair Helen told me of their stealth,

Of this their purpose hither to this wood;

And I in fury hither follow'd them,

Fair Helena in fancy following me.

But, my good lord, I wot not by what power,—

But by some power it is,—my love to Hermia,

Melted as the snow—seems to me now

As the remembrance of an idle gawd

Which in my childhood I did dote upon:

And all the faith, the virtue of my heart,

The object and the pleasure of mine eye,

Is only Helena. To her, my lord,

Was I betroth'd ere I saw Hermia:

But, like a sickness, did I loathe this food;

But, as in health, come to my natural taste,

Now I do wish it, love it, long for it,

And will for evermore be true to it.

THESEUS

Fair lovers, you are fortunately met:

Of this discourse we more will hear anon.—

Egeus, I will overbear your will;

For in the temple, by and by with us,

These couples shall eternally be knit.

And, for the morning now is something worn,

Our purpos'd hunting shall be set aside.—

Away with us to Athens, three and three,

We'll hold a feast in great solemnity.—

Come, Hippolyta.

[Exeunt THESEUS, HIPPOLYTA, EGEUS, and Train.]

DEMETRIUS

These things seem small and undistinguishable,

Like far-off mountains turnèd into clouds.

HERMIA

Methinks I see these things with parted eye,

When every thing seems double.

HELENA

          So methinks:

And I have found Demetrius like a jewel.

Mine own, and not mine own.

DEMETRIUS

          It seems to me

That yet we sleep, we dream.—Do not you think

The duke was here, and bid us follow him?

HERMIA

Yea, and my father.

HELENA

          And Hippolyta.

LYSANDER

And he did bid us follow to the temple.

DEMETRIUS

Why, then, we are awake: let's follow him;

And by the way let us recount our dreams.

[Exeunt.]

[As they go out, BOTTOM awakes.]

BOTTOM

When my cue comes, call me, and I will answer. My next is 'Most fair Pyramus.'—Heigh-ho!—Peter Quince! Flute, the bellows-mender! Snout, the tinker! Starveling! God's my life, stol'n hence, and left me asleep! I have had a most rare vision. I have had a dream—past the wit of man to say what dream it was.—Man is but an ass if he go about to expound this dream. Methought I was—there is no man can tell what. Methought I was, and methought I had,—but man is but a patched fool, if he will offer to say what methought I had. The eye of man hath not heard, the ear of man hath not seen; man's hand is not able to taste, his tongue to conceive, nor his heart to report, what my dream was. I will get Peter Quince to write a ballad of this dream: it shall be called Bottom's Dream, because it hath no bottom; and I will sing it in the latter end of a play, before the duke: peradventure, to make it the more gracious, I shall sing it at her death.

[Exit.]

SCENE II.   Athens.   A Room in QUINCE'S House

[Enter QUINCE, FLUTE, SNOUT, and STARVELING.]

QUINCE

Have you sent to Bottom's house? is he come home yet?

STARVELING

He cannot be heard of. Out of doubt, he is transported.

FLUTE

If he come not, then the play is marred; it goes not forward, doth it?

QUINCE

It is not possible: you have not a man in all Athens able to discharge Pyramus but he.

FLUTE

No; he hath simply the best wit of any handicraft man in Athens.

QUINCE

Yea, and the best person too: and he is a very paramour for a sweet voice.

FLUTE

You must say paragon: a paramour is, God bless us, a thing of naught.

[Enter SNUG.]

SNUG

Masters, the duke is coming from the temple; and there is two or three lords and ladies more married: if our sport had gone forward, we had all been made men.

FLUTE

O sweet bully Bottom! Thus hath he lost sixpence a day during his life; he could not have 'scaped sixpence a-day; an the duke had not given him sixpence a-day for playing Pyramus, I'll be hanged; he would have deserved it: sixpence a-day in Pyramus, or nothing.

[Enter BOTTOM.]

BOTTOM

Where are these lads? where are these hearts?

QUINCE

Bottom!—O most courageous day! O most happy hour!

BOTTOM

Masters, I am to discourse wonders: but ask me not what; for if I tell you, I am not true Athenian. I will tell you everything, right as it fell out.

QUINCE

Let us hear, sweet Bottom.

BOTTOM

Not a word of me. All that I will tell you is, that the duke hath dined. Get your apparel together; good strings to your beards, new ribbons to your pumps; meet presently at the palace; every man look over his part; for the short and the long is, our play is preferred. In any case, let Thisby have clean linen; and let not him that plays the lion pare his nails, for they shall hang out for the lion's claws. And, most dear actors, eat no onions nor garlick, for we are to utter sweet breath; and I do not doubt but to hear them say it is a sweet comedy. No more words: away! go; away!

[Exeunt.]

A Midsummer Night's Dream

ACT V

SCENE I. Athens. An Apartment in the Palace of THESEUS

[Enter THESEUS, HIPPOLYTA, PHILOSTRATE, Lords, and Attendants.]

HIPPOLYTA

'Tis strange, my Theseus, that these lovers speak of.

THESEUS

More strange than true. I never may believe

These antique fables, nor these fairy toys.

Lovers and madmen have such seething brains,

Such shaping fantasies, that apprehend

More than cool reason ever comprehends.

The lunatic, the lover, and the poet

Are of imagination all compact:

One sees more devils than vast hell can hold;

That is the madman: the lover, all as frantic,

Sees Helen's beauty in a brow of Egypt:

The poet's eye, in a fine frenzy rolling,

Doth glance from heaven to earth, from earth to heaven;

And as imagination bodies forth

The forms of things unknown, the poet's pen

Turns them to shapes, and gives to airy nothing

A local habitation and a name.

Such tricks hath strong imagination,

That, if it would but apprehend some joy,

It comprehends some bringer of that joy;

Or in the night, imagining some fear,

How easy is a bush supposed a bear?

HIPPOLYTA

But all the story of the night told over,

And all their minds transfigur'd so together,

More witnesseth than fancy's images,

And grows to something of great constancy;

But, howsoever, strange and admirable.

[Enter LYSANDER, DEMETRIUS, HERMIA, and HELENA.]

THESEUS

Here come the lovers, full of joy and mirth.—

Joy, gentle friends! joy and fresh days of love

Accompany your hearts!

LYSANDER

                    More than to us

Wait in your royal walks, your board, your bed!

THESEUS

Come now; what masques, what dances shall we have,

To wear away this long age of three hours

Between our after-supper and bed-time?

Where is our usual manager of mirth?

What revels are in hand? Is there no play

To ease the anguish of a torturing hour?

Call Philostrate.

PHILOSTRATE

                  Here, mighty Theseus.

THESEUS

Say, what abridgment have you for this evening?

What masque? what music? How shall we beguile

The lazy time, if not with some delight?

PHILOSTRATE

There is a brief how many sports are ripe;

Make choice of which your highness will see first.

[Giving a paper]

THESEUS

[Reads]

  'The battle with the Centaurs, to be sung

    By an Athenian eunuch to the harp.'

We'll none of that: that have I told my love,

In glory of my kinsman Hercules.

'The riot of the tipsy Bacchanals,

Tearing the Thracian singer in their rage.'

That is an old device, and it was play'd

When I from Thebes came last a conqueror.

'The thrice three Muses mourning for the death

Of learning, late deceas'd in beggary.'

That is some satire, keen and critical,

Not sorting with a nuptial ceremony.

'A tedious brief scene of young Pyramus

And his love Thisbe; very tragical mirth.'

Merry and tragical! tedious and brief!

That is hot ice and wondrous strange snow.

How shall we find the concord of this discord?

PHILOSTRATE

A play there is, my lord, some ten words long,

Which is as brief as I have known a play;

But by ten words, my lord, it is too long,

Which makes it tedious: for in all the play

There is not one word apt, one player fitted:

And tragical, my noble lord, it is;

For Pyramus therein doth kill himself:

Which when I saw rehears'd, I must confess,

Made mine eyes water; but more merry tears

The passion of loud laughter never shed.

THESEUS

What are they that do play it?

PHILOSTRATE

Hard-handed men that work in Athens here,

Which never labour'd in their minds till now;

And now have toil'd their unbreath'd memories

With this same play against your nuptial.

THESEUS

And we will hear it.

PHILOSTRATE

        No, my noble lord,

It is not for you: I have heard it over,

And it is nothing, nothing in the world;

Unless you can find sport in their intents,

Extremely stretch'd and conn'd with cruel pain,

To do you service.

THESEUS

        I will hear that play;

For never anything can be amiss

When simpleness and duty tender it.

Go, bring them in: and take your places, ladies.

[Exit PHILOSTRATE.]

HIPPOLYTA

I love not to see wretchedness o'er-charged,

And duty in his service perishing.

THESEUS

Why, gentle sweet, you shall see no such thing.

HIPPOLYTA

He says they can do nothing in this kind.

THESEUS

The kinder we, to give them thanks for nothing.

Our sport shall be to take what they mistake:

And what poor duty cannot do,

Noble respect takes it in might, not merit.

Where I have come, great clerks have purposed

To greet me with premeditated welcomes;

Where I have seen them shiver and look pale,

Make periods in the midst of sentences,

Throttle their practis'd accent in their fears,

And, in conclusion, dumbly have broke off,

Not paying me a welcome. Trust me, sweet,

Out of this silence yet I pick'd a welcome;

And in the modesty of fearful duty

I read as much as from the rattling tongue

Of saucy and audacious eloquence.

Love, therefore, and tongue-tied simplicity

In least speak most to my capacity.

[Enter PHILOSTRATE.]

PHILOSTRATE

So please your grace, the prologue is address'd.

THESEUS

Let him approach.

[Flourish of trumpets. Enter PROLOGUE.]

PROLOGUE

'If we offend, it is with our good will.

   That you should think, we come not to offend,

But with good will. To show our simple skill,

   That is the true beginning of our end.

Consider then, we come but in despite.

   We do not come, as minding to content you,

Our true intent is. All for your delight

   We are not here. That you should here repent you,

The actors are at hand: and, by their show,

You shall know all that you are like to know,'

THESEUS

This fellow doth not stand upon points.

LYSANDER

He hath rid his prologue like a rough colt; he knows not the stop. A good moral, my lord: it is not enough to speak, but to speak true.

HIPPOLYTA

Indeed he hath played on this prologue like a child on a recorder; a sound, but not in government.

THESEUS

His speech was like a tangled chain; nothing impaired, but all disordered. Who is next?

[Enter PYRAMUS and THISBE, WALL, MOONSHINE, and LION, as in dumb show.]

PROLOGUE

Gentles, perchance you wonder at this show;

　But wonder on, till truth make all things plain.

This man is Pyramus, if you would know;

　This beauteous lady Thisby is certain.

This man, with lime and rough-cast, doth present

　Wall, that vile Wall which did these lovers sunder;

And through Wall's chink, poor souls, they are content

　To whisper, at the which let no man wonder.

This man, with lanthorn, dog, and bush of thorn,

　Presenteth Moonshine: for, if you will know,

By moonshine did these lovers think no scorn

    To meet at Ninus' tomb, there, there to woo.

This grisly beast, which by name Lion hight,

The trusty Thisby, coming first by night,

Did scare away, or rather did affright;

And as she fled, her mantle she did fall;

    Which Lion vile with bloody mouth did stain:

Anon comes Pyramus, sweet youth, and tall,

    And finds his trusty Thisby's mantle slain;

Whereat with blade, with bloody blameful blade,

    He bravely broach'd his boiling bloody breast;

And Thisby, tarrying in mulberry shade,

    His dagger drew, and died. For all the rest,

Let Lion, Moonshine, Wall, and lovers twain,

At large discourse while here they do remain.

[Exeunt PROLOGUE, THISBE, LION, and MOONSHINE.]

THESEUS

I wonder if the lion be to speak.

DEMETRIUS

No wonder, my lord: one lion may, when many asses do.

WALL

In this same interlude it doth befall

That I, one Snout by name, present a wall:

And such a wall as I would have you think

That had in it a crannied hole or chink,

Through which the lovers, Pyramus and Thisby,

Did whisper often very secretly.

This loam, this rough-cast, and this stone, doth show

That I am that same wall; the truth is so:

And this the cranny is, right and sinister,

Through which the fearful lovers are to whisper.

THESEUS

Would you desire lime and hair to speak better?

DEMETRIUS

It is the wittiest partition that ever I heard discourse, my lord.

THESEUS

Pyramus draws near the wall; silence.

[Enter PYRAMUS.]

PYRAMUS

O grim-look'd night! O night with hue so black!

  O night, which ever art when day is not!

O night, O night, alack, alack, alack,

  I fear my Thisby's promise is forgot!—

And thou, O wall, O sweet, O lovely wall,

That stand'st between her father's ground and mine;

Thou wall, O wall, O sweet and lovely wall,

Show me thy chink, to blink through with mine eyne.

[WALL holds up his fingers.]

Thanks, courteous wall: Jove shield thee well for this!

But what see what see I? No Thisby do I see.

O wicked wall, through whom I see no bliss,

Curs'd be thy stones for thus deceiving me!

THESEUS

The wall, methinks, being sensible, should curse again.

PYRAMUS

No, in truth, sir, he should not. 'Deceiving me' is Thisby's cue: she is to enter now, and I am to spy her through the wall. You shall see it will fall pat as I told you.—Yonder she comes.

[Enter THISBE.]

THISBE

O wall, full often hast thou heard my moans,

For parting my fair Pyramus and me:

My cherry lips have often kiss'd thy stones:

Thy stones with lime and hair knit up in thee.

PYRAMUS

I see a voice; now will I to the chink,

To spy an I can hear my Thisby's face.

Thisby!

THISBE

My love! thou art my love, I think.

PYRAMUS

Think what thou wilt, I am thy lover's grace;

And like Limander am I trusty still.

THISBE

And I like Helen, till the fates me kill.

PYRAMUS

Not Shafalus to Procrus was so true.

THISBE

As Shafalus to Procrus, I to you.

PYRAMUS

O, kiss me through the hole of this vile wall

.

THISBE

I kiss the wall's hole, not your lips at all.

PYRAMUS

Wilt thou at Ninny's tomb meet me straightway?

THISBE

'Tide life, 'tide death, I come without delay.

WALL

Thus have I, wall, my part discharged so;

And, being done, thus Wall away doth go.

[Exeunt WALL, PYRAMUS and THISBE.]

THESEUS

Now is the mural down between the two neighbours.

DEMETRIUS

No remedy, my lord, when walls are so wilful to hear without warning.

HIPPOLYTA

This is the silliest stuff that ever I heard.

THESEUS

The best in this kind are but shadows; and the worst are no worse, if imagination amend them.

HIPPOLYTA

It must be your imagination then, and not theirs.

THESEUS

If we imagine no worse of them than they of themselves, they may pass for excellent men. Here come two noble beasts in, a moon and a lion.

[Enter LION and MOONSHINE.]

LION

You, ladies, you, whose gentle hearts do fear

The smallest monstrous mouse that creeps on floor,

May now, perchance, both quake and tremble here,

When lion rough in wildest rage doth roar.

Then know that I, one Snug the joiner, am

A lion fell, nor else no lion's dam:

For, if I should as lion come in strife

Into this place, 'twere pity on my life.

THESEUS

A very gentle beast, and of a good conscience.

DEMETRIUS

The very best at a beast, my lord, that e'er I saw.

LYSANDER

This lion is a very fox for his valour.

THESEUS

True; and a goose for his discretion.

DEMETRIUS

Not so, my lord; for his valour cannot carry his discretion, and the fox carries the goose.

THESEUS

His discretion, I am sure, cannot carry his valour; for the goose carries not the fox. It is well; leave it to his discretion, and let us listen to the moon.

MOONSHINE

This lanthorn doth the hornèd moon present:

DEMETRIUS

He should have worn the horns on his head.

THESEUS

He is no crescent, and his horns are invisible within the circumference.

MOONSHINE

This lanthorn doth the hornèd moon present;

Myself the man i' the moon do seem to be.

THESEUS

This is the greatest error of all the rest: the man should be put into the lantern. How is it else the man i' the moon?

DEMETRIUS

He dares not come there for the candle: for, you see, it is already in snuff.

HIPPOLYTA

I am aweary of this moon: would he would change!

THESEUS

It appears, by his small light of discretion, that he is in the wane: but yet, in courtesy, in all reason, we must stay the time.

LYSANDER

Proceed, moon.

MOON

All that I have to say, is to tell you that the lantern is the moon; I, the man i' the moon; this thorn-bush, my thorn-bush; and this dog, my dog.

DEMETRIUS

Why, all these should be in the lantern; for all these are in the moon. But silence; here comes Thisbe.

[Enter THISBE.]

THISBE

This is old Ninny's tomb. Where is my love?

LION

Oh!

[The LION roars.—THISBE runs off.]

DEMETRIUS

Well roared, lion.

THESEUS

Well run, Thisbe.

HIPPOLYTA

Well shone, moon.—Truly, the moon shines with a good grace.

[The LION tears THISBE'S Mantle, and exit.]

THESEUS

Well moused, lion.

DEMETRIUS

And so comes Pyramus.

LYSANDER

And then the lion vanishes.

[Enter PYRAMUS.]

PYRAMUS

Sweet moon, I thank thee for thy sunny beams;

   I thank thee, moon, for shining now so bright:

For, by thy gracious golden, glittering streams,

   I trust to take of truest Thisby's sight.

      But stay;—O spite!

      But mark,—poor knight,

     What dreadful dole is here!

      Eyes, do you see?

      How can it be?

    O dainty duck! O dear!

      Thy mantle good,

     What! stained with blood?

    Approach, ye furies fell!

      O fates! come, come;

      Cut thread and thrum;

    Quail, rush, conclude, and quell!

THESEUS

This passion, and the death of a dear friend, would go near to make a man look sad.

HIPPOLYTA

Beshrew my heart, but I pity the man.

PYRAMUS

O wherefore, nature, didst thou lions frame?

 Since lion vile hath here deflower'd my dear;

Which is—no, no—which was the fairest dame

 That liv'd, that lov'd, that lik'd, that look'd with cheer.

 Come, tears, confound;

 Out, sword, and wound

 The pap of Pyramus:

 Ay, that left pap,

 Where heart doth hop:—

 Thus die I, thus, thus, thus.

 Now am I dead,

 Now am I fled;

 My soul is in the sky:

 Tongue, lose thy light!

 Moon, take thy flight!

 Now die, die, die, die, die.

[Dies. Exit MOONSHINE.]

DEMETRIUS

No die, but an ace, for him; for he is but one.

LYSANDER

Less than an ace, man; for he is dead; he is nothing.

THESEUS

With the help of a surgeon he might yet recover and prove an ass.

HIPPOLYTA

How chance moonshine is gone before Thisbe comes back and finds her lover?

THESEUS

She will find him by starlight.—Here she comes; and her passion ends the play.

[Enter THISBE.]

HIPPOLYTA

Methinks she should not use a long one for such a Pyramus: I hope she will be brief.

DEMETRIUS

A mote will turn the balance, which Pyramus, which Thisbe, is the better.

LYSANDER

She hath spied him already with those sweet eyes.

DEMETRIUS

And thus she moans, videlicet.—

THISBE

    Asleep, my love?

    What, dead, my dove?

O Pyramus, arise,

    Speak, speak. Quite dumb?

    Dead, dead? A tomb

Must cover thy sweet eyes.

    These lily lips,

    This cherry nose,

These yellow cowslip cheeks,

    Are gone, are gone:

    Lovers, make moan!

His eyes were green as leeks.

    O Sisters Three,

    Come, come to me,

With hands as pale as milk;

    Lay them in gore,

    Since you have shore

With shears his thread of silk.

    Tongue, not a word:—

    Come, trusty sword;

Come, blade, my breast imbrue;

    And farewell, friends:—

    Thus Thisbe ends;

Adieu, adieu, adieu.

[Dies.]

THESEUS

Moonshine and lion are left to bury the dead.

DEMETRIUS

Ay, and wall too.

BOTTOM

No, I assure you; the wall is down that parted their fathers. Will it please you to see the epilogue, or to hear a Bergomask dance between two of our company?

THESEUS

No epilogue, I pray you; for your play needs no excuse. Never excuse; for when the players are all dead there need none to be blamed. Marry, if he that writ it had played Pyramus, and hang'd himself in Thisbe's garter, it would have been a fine tragedy: and so it is, truly; and very notably discharged. But come, your Bergomask; let your epilogue alone.

[Here a dance of Clowns.]

The iron tongue of midnight hath told twelve:—

Lovers, to bed; 'tis almost fairy time.

I fear we shall out-sleep the coming morn,

As much as we this night have overwatch'd.

This palpable-gross play hath well beguil'd

The heavy gait of night.—Sweet friends, to bed.—

A fortnight hold we this solemnity,

In nightly revels and new jollity.

[Exeunt.]

SCENE II

[Enter PUCK.]

PUCK

Now the hungry lion roars,

 And the wolf behowls the moon;

Whilst the heavy ploughman snores,

 All with weary task fordone.

Now the wasted brands do glow,

 Whilst the scritch-owl, scritching loud,

Puts the wretch that lies in woe

 In remembrance of a shroud.

Now it is the time of night

 That the graves, all gaping wide,

Every one lets forth its sprite,

 In the church-way paths to glide:

And we fairies, that do run

 By the triple Hecate's team

From the presence of the sun,

 Following darkness like a dream,

Now are frolic; not a mouse

 Shall disturb this hallow'd house:

I am sent with broom before,

  To sweep the dust behind the door.

[Enter OBERON and TITANIA, with their Train.]

OBERON

  Through the house give glimmering light,

    By the dead and drowsy fire:

  Every elf and fairy sprite

    Hop as light as bird from brier:

  And this ditty, after me,

  Sing and dance it trippingly.

TITANIA

  First, rehearse your song by rote,

    To each word a warbling note;

  Hand in hand, with fairy grace,

  Will we sing, and bless this place.

[Song and Dance.]

OBERON

  Now, until the break of day,

  Through this house each fairy stray,

  To the best bride-bed will we,

  Which by us shall blessèd be;

  And the issue there create

Ever shall be fortunate.

So shall all the couples three

Ever true in loving be;

And the blots of Nature's hand

Shall not in their issue stand:

Never mole, hare-lip, nor scar,

Nor mark prodigious, such as are

Despised in nativity,

Shall upon their children be.—

With this field-dew consecrate,

Every fairy take his gate;

And each several chamber bless,

Through this palace, with sweet peace;

E'er shall it in safety rest,

And the owner of it blest.

Trip away:

Make no stay:

Meet me all by break of day.

[Exeunt OBERON, TITANIA, and Train.]

PUCK

If we shadows have offended,

Think but this,—and all is mended,—

That you have but slumber'd here

While these visions did appear.

And this weak and idle theme,

No more yielding but a dream,

Gentles, do not reprehend;

If you pardon, we will mend.

And, as I am an honest Puck,

If we have unearnèd luck

Now to 'scape the serpent's tongue,

We will make amends ere long;

Else the Puck a liar call:

So, good night unto you all.

Give me your hands, if we be friends,

And Robin shall restore amends.

[Exit.]

33490736R00077

Made in the USA
Lexington, KY
26 June 2014